LISTEN, WHAT TALES TELL...

AF568925

SAKSHI

Copyright © Sakshi
All Rights Reserved.

This book has been published with all efforts taken to make the material error-free after the consent of the author. However, the author and the publisher do not assume and hereby disclaim any liability to any party for any loss, damage, or disruption caused by errors or omissions, whether such errors or omissions result from negligence, accident, or any other cause.

While every effort has been made to avoid any mistake or omission, this publication is being sold on the condition and understanding that neither the author nor the publishers or printers would be liable in any manner to any person by reason of any mistake or omission in this publication or for any action taken or omitted to be taken or advice rendered or accepted on the basis of this work. For any defect in printing or binding the publishers will be liable only to replace the defective copy by another copy of this work then available.

I dedicate this book to the people who came into my life

and added new and beautiful chapters in it.

Contents

Preface

Welcome my readers in the roller coaster ride of so many fictional characters created by me. The names and the places might be unknown to you but their feelings, struggles, ups and downs; and their stories will look familiar to you all, as we all have faced them in our lives at some point. These short stories are not exactly the fairy tales but your thinking and viewpoint may make them so. I hope you will find something good and valuable thought my stories. I wish that you will enjoy reading each and every story as much as I enjoyed writing them.

Acknowledgements

For me, acknowledgment is the best part of the book. Here I can express my gratitude towards the important persons in my life. I owe this book to the people in my life who are always there for me, who taught, guided and mentored me.

I wanted to thank my parents, who encouraged me, taught me, made me understand that to learn from our mistakes is a good thing and to support me.

I would never be able to grow in a better direction without the support and guidence of my teacher – Amit sir. Thank you so much sir, for always solving my problems and taught me various precious life lessons.

Without the support of my friends and their weird encouraging speeches, I wouldn't be able to write this book.

Thank you everyone once again!

CHAPTER ONE

Blossom

"Children, animals and plants all require our full attention, care and love."

Rihan was a ten years old naughty kid, lived with his elder sister Riya in the valley of Himachal Pradesh. He used to pluck flowers, buds and leaves from the neighbor's house, gardens, private farms, and also from his school. He used to play with the flowers for some time and then he crushed them and threw them on the streets. His neighbors stopped him several times but he never listened to them and angrily plucked the whole newly planted plant from its roots. Rihan didn't like to be interrupted by anyone. He always took out his rage on the innocent little plants and flowers.

The actions of Rihan became intolerable by the people, so they came to Riya to complain about Rihan and his deeds. Riya was shocked after listening to all the complaints. She loved growing plants and taking care of them. At first, she didn't believe them but one day, she saw that her brother was plucking flowers from the neighbor's house and one by one he plucked all the petals of a rose flower. She was stunned to see him like this. She wasn't able to understand his rage. On that day, she decided to change the mindset of her younger brother. At one morning of the winters, she knocked the door of Rihan's room and entered. She was holding a rose which she found fallen in the garden of her colony. "Get up Rihan. Look what I have brought for you," she said. Rihan opened his eyes a little and when he saw a flower he got up and sat straight on the bed. "Do you like flowers?" Riya asked. "Yes," Rihan said and forwarded his hands to take the flower but Riya moved her hand back. "Give it to me “, he said. "I will, but first you tell me, do you want to plant a plant, so that you will play with the flowers all day?" Riya asked. Rihan thought once then agreed. They went into a nursery and Rihan selected a small grafted rose plant. He planted the rose into an earthen pot and watered it. He started giving his most of the time to the rose plant. But the plant didn't grow further. Slowly the leaves started shedding off from the plant. He asked his sister about the reason for it. His sister smiled and said," do whatever you are doing till now. Soon the new leaves will emerge from the plant. Don't worry." Initially he didn't believe her but he had no other option so he watered the plant every day. One day he noticed, some small leaves had started growing. Rihan became so happy and gave all his time and care to that plant. Gradually, the plant grew and a bud emerged from a branch. When Rihan saw the bud, he thought when it became a fully matured flower, he would pluck and keep it in his favourite book. And when the rose bloomed, its big and exquisitely crimson petals gained the attention of Rihan. He couldn't let his eyes off the flower. The rose was the prize of his hard work and care towards the plant. At that time, he realized how brutal his acts were! He touched the flower smoothly and carefully and promised to himself that he would never pluck any flower. Riya was carefully observing everything and when Rihan didn't pluck the rose, she smiled and hugged her little brother.

Because of that plant, Rihan also blossomed into a caring and loving child.

CHAPTER TWO

Learning

***"*"We should try to spread happiness but first of all we must be happy with ourselves."*"**

There was a man named Tejas, who was in his late thirties, lived with his wife and a daughter. He used to be a kind and helpful person. But one day his father met with an accident in Delhi. He asked for the leaves in the office but due to the lots of work and chances to get a big new project, his leave application was denied. So, he resigned and went to see his father. His father was in very critical condition and for his surgery a large amount of money was required. As he had no job, he couldn't get a loan from any bank. He broke all his FDs but unfortunately, he wasn't able to collect the total amount for the surgery. So, he borrowed the rest of the money for a jeweler and gave him his wife's jewelry as grantee. In spite of all these efforts, he couldn't save his father. Tejas, who once helped everyone now he himself became helpless. He lost his father, he lost his job, and he only left with lots of borrowed money. He couldn't get a new job anywhere. Gradually he became an irritated father, an angry husband and a depressed person. He started roaming in the streets to avoid his family. He came home late at night to ignore conflicts.

One evening he was sitting on a bench in the park. His eyes caught the attention of a kid who nearly started walking. Tejas started observing each and every move of the kid. The kid faltered in every step but he tried again and again to make his steps perfect and steady. The kid picked up a fallen flower and came towards Tejas, slowly and gave him the flower with a heartwarming smile. Tejas once thought but took the flower and smiled back. The kid became happy by the response of Tejas and started playing again in the park. But suddenly, the kid fell and started crying. Tejas quickly got up and moved towards the kid to help him. But the actions of the kid made him stop on his spot. At that moment, Tejas learned the best life lesson from that kid. He saw that the kid stopped crying and forgot all his pain when he caught the attention of a flying butterfly. The kid got up again and followed the butterfly and giggled. Tejas also smiled seeing the kid and this time he smiled from his heart.

That unknown little kid made Tejas smile and made him realize that no matter how many times you fall in life or fail in life. There is always something which gives you hope, like the butterfly gave hope to the kid who stood again on his feet to start again and forgot all his problems.

CHAPTER THREE

Sweet Suspense

"Generally, suspense increases our adrenaline rush but sometimes when some suspense solves, it makes us laugh at our silly thinking."

It was a pleasant morning in March 1989. Kishor got up early and went for a morning walk. He had a cloth shop and lived with his wife and three children. Kishor didn't give much of his time to his family; he was generally busy in building his business only. His elder son, Vijay was 22 years old and worked in the private sector. Kishor and his wife Parvati were looking for a suitable girl for Vijay. His second son, Atul was 15 years old and he loved his younger sister, Shashi a lot. Parvati was usually a very humble person but when she got to know that her husband was eating sweets, then no one could match her anger. Kishor was a diabetic patient, not the serious one, but his wife was very serious to keep him miles away from the sweets and chocolates. Kishor understood the caring nature behind her anger but he didn't like to see her face full of anger because of him. So, he ate chocolates secretly, which he kept behind the photo of the Lord Ganesh in his shop. And to balance this, he got up early in the morning and went on the morning walk. Also, he used to do yoga and exercise after walking. He loved to eat chocolates and he knew, no matter how hard he workout, his wife would never allow him to eat chocolates and he couldn't live happily without sweets or chocolates, so he vowed to himself that he would only eat one chocolate per day and work out hard to counter the effect of the sugar. His cloth shop was outside his house and to enter the house, one had to pass through his shop as it was the only way. He opened the shop around 9 in the morning when Vijay left for his job, Atul and Shashi were in the school and his wife was in the house and generally, she didn't come to the shop early in the morning. After opening the shop, he lit up the *diya* and prayed to God and then he lifted the photo frame of Lord Ganesh slightly and saw that only six chocolates were there. He got confused because he definitely remembered that there were seven chocolates till yesterday. But except him no one knew about it, so there was no one to be accused. He picked one chocolate and tried to remembered again but he was sure there must be seven chocolates till yesterday. He was afraid of his wife, if she got to know about this, she would freak out. There was nothing robbed from the shop which indicated that someone from the family had eaten the chocolate. So, he thought he would keep an eye on everyone tonight and silently prayed to God that his wife did not get to know about it. Eventually, time passed and, in the night, everyone went to their respective rooms to sleep. Shashi used to sleep next to her father. Kishor was unable to sleep but when he noticed that after sometime, Shashi got up from the bed, he partially closed his eyes. He couldn't believe that Shashi could take chocolates from his shop. She was just 11 years old. He was in shock and thought if she wanted to eat chocolates then why not she directly told him. With a heavy heart he followed her but he saw that she didn't go in the direction of the shop, instead she went in the room of Atul. For a second, he relaxed and felt happy but curiosity captured him immediately. *Why did Shashi go into the room of Atul late at night?* He went near the room of Atul and peeped into the room as the door was ajar. He saw that Shashi was waking up her brother and told him that she wasn't able to sleep. Atul got up and sat on the bed and folded his legs and Shashi put her head on his thighs and laid down on the bed. Atul put his hands on her head and started singing a lullaby — the same lullaby which Kishor's mother used to sign. After seeing all this, Kishor couldn't control his tears. He realized how much he had been busy with his work and in extending his business that he completely forgot about his family's small happiness. He thought he would go out with his family every Sundays, now onwards. He was returning to his room when he noticed that the dim light of the torch was coming from his shop, adrenaline rushed into his blood streams. He moved quickly but carefully towards the shop. He saw that his elder son, Vijay was trespassing on the *saree* section of the shop. Kishor got confused. *Why did he look for a saree? For Parvati?* But it couldn't make any sense. He didn't interrupt Vijay but watched him carefully. When Kishor was convinced that there was no harm to the chocolates from Vijay, he left Vijay with his *saree* and went back to his room. He thought he would ask him next morning about the *saree*.

In the morning, the first thing in Kishor's to-do list was to interrogate Vijay. He went into Vijay's room and asked about yesterday. Vijay went blank and nervous at the same time. Vijay hesitated and told that he was looking for the *saree* for his friend Pallavi and his mother knew about it. Kishor didn't say anything for a few minutes but then he recalled last night when he thought about giving his time to his family and now, he got an opportunity to work this out. Then, Kishor asked Vijay if he wanted them to meet Pallavi's family and Vijay nodded and slowly said that he and his mother assumed that he would disagree about it. Kishor smiled and hugged his son and told him that he would talk to Parvati. When he told everything to Parvati, she agreed happily to meet Pallavi's family but she asked Kishor what he was doing at the shop late at night. Kishor hesitated and then said that he went into the kitchen to drink water and then he saw a dim light coming from the shop. Parvati wasn't convinced but she let the topic go. That day, there were no missing chocolates. He thought he must had forgotten the counting's of the chocolates.

One night he saw that his wife was not in the bed and after a few minutes she didn't come back. He went in search of Parvati; he saw that the light of the shop was on and Parvati was sitting on the counter of the shop and... and she was eating the **CHOCOLATES**! He imagined that if Parvati got to know about these chocolates, then that situation would cause havoc in the house but this was just an opposite situation. She was enjoying eating *his* chocolates. He took the steps to confront his wife and when she saw him, she was shocked as if she was hiding all those chocolates in the shop for the whole time. She was not looking angry at all, so Kishor asked why she was eating chocolates like this. She flushed and then said that she also liked chocolates but she didn't eat them because if she ate them then he also wanted to eat them which was not good for his health. And one day, she saw him taking the chocolate, from behind the photo frame. On that night, she made a plan to teach a lesson to him and also to eat chocolates. So, she ate the chocolate for the first time from the shop a few days back. Kishor laughed out loud after listening to the whole story. Kishor said that he thought she would be mad when she got to know about this. Parvati smiled and said that she was not mad, she only cared about his health.

Another day was Friday, Kishor brought a big box of chocolates and the whole family happily celebrated the weak end and enjoyed the whole story of "sweet suspense", told by Kishor and Parvati.

CHAPTER FOUR

Kheer

"" We can show gratitude just by doing little efforts.""

Leela was a well graduated and a married woman. She was a house wife and she loved her family. But in spite of being well educated, people know her as Rajat's wife or as Mrs. Sharma. There was no doubt that she was a supporting wife and loving daughter in-law, but the truth was, she lost her own identity. Rajat was also a supporting husband. He usually told her to do a job or do whatever she wanted to do in her life but her mother-in-law was a patient of Alzheimer's and due to this she needed a familiar face around her along with a nurse 24×7. So, Leela gave up all her dreams and dedicated all her time to her family. She never complained about it but at some point, she felt disconnected with the outside world. She also wanted to spend some quality time with her friends and also wanted to go out for movies or dinner with her husband. Rajat understood her completely, that's why he took the few days off from the office at the interval of two or three months and spent time with his mother and wife.

One day Rajat noticed that Leela was upset and riding in her own train of thoughts. "What's wrong?" Rajat asked. "Nothing. I am just tired. I just want to relax and do nothing," she said. Rajat recognized the answer for a few minutes and then said," so take a nap. I will go to the office late. I am sure my boss will understand. He is a nice person." Leela didn't say anything.

She just smiled as if she was too tired to explain further and left the room. Rajat went to see her mother and asked for the updates from the nurse. Nurse said that she was stable as the medications were quite effective. Rajat kissed her mother on the forehead and sat beside her. " These medications are effective but I am bored of this room. I rested all day, doing nothing," Rajat's mother complained. "I will tell Leela to play old songs of Dilip Kumar for you. Okay?" Rajat said, smiling. His mother laughed a little and said, "she is very kind to me. We are lucky to have her as a part of our family. Do something for her, make her happy. She looks upset so many times."

" You are right, mother. I should do something special for her. Oh yes! Her birthday is coming, so that will be the perfect occasion to do something for her. But please don't tell her mother. It will be a surprise for her."

"I will not tell her anything," his mother promised.

2 days later, Leela became 35 years old. But she was not excited for her birthday. Rajat's plan was ready to surprise Leela and he was quite excited. He hid all his excitement and causally wished Leela. She smiled and said thank you and served his breakfast as he was running late for his office. He went into his office and called Amrita (best friend of Leela) and told her about his plan. She agreed quickly and hung up. In the evening, he went to the house of his friend Utkarsh, who studied with Rajat. Utkarsh was unmarried and as it was not a weekend, he was in his house. Rajat brought a packet of milk, rice, sugar and dry fruits to the Utkarsh's house. Rajat hugged him and said, "Today is my wife's birthday and I want to surprise her by making Kheer. So, I am going to make this kheer in your Kitchen. "Thanks brother, for your help." "But I didn't say yes to your surprise plan," Utkarsh said, teasingly. "Oh! You are my best friend, I don't need any permission," Rajat said and they both laughed at the same time. Without wasting any time, Rajat washed the rice with fresh water and soaked them for 15 to 20 minutes. Meanwhile he let the milk boil in the saucepan and he stirred it occasionally to avoid burning. After a few minutes he took out 2 tablespoons of milk into a bowl and added a few saffron strands into the milk and kept it aside. He then added the rinsed rice into the boiling milk and let them cook when the rice was halved cooked, he added sugar into the milk and let it cook onto a medium flame. He stirred it at the proper interval. When the milk condensed, he added chopped cashew, sliced pistachios, raisins and then added saffron dissolved milk in it. The kheer looked delicious and its aroma captured the attention of Utkarsh. " You improved your cooking skills, Rajat. It smells delicious, can I taste it?" Utkarsh asked. "Of Course, you can eat this. Go get ready, we are leaving in 10 minutes," Rajat said. " Sorry friend, I am not coming. Today is a party at my boss's place and I have to go there," Utkarsh said. "Oh, okay but I am leaving this Kheer for you too in the fridge," Rajat said. Utkarsh hugged him tightly and said, "you are the best brother." Rajat laughed and then he cleaned his lunch box and poured half of the Kheer and left. He reached home and rang the bell. Leela opened the door and offered a glass of water. He refused, so she tried to take the lunch box but

Rajat didn't want to give it to her. He was about to say something but the main door's bell rang and Leela went to open the door. Rajat sighed and went into the kitchen and put the lunch box on the slab. "**SURPRISE,**" said all Leela's school and college friends. Leela was shocked and couldn't control her tears. She was seeing all of them after so many years. She hugged all her friends and looked towards Rajat. He was standing at the kitchen's door and he was also looking at her. She went near him and said, "Thank you so much". He hugged her and wished her again. Amrita shouted, "it's cake cutting time." Leela asked to wait 10 minutes and she went into the room. After a few minutes she came out with Rajat's mother and said, "now it's cake cutting time." They all smiled and she cut the cake and the party went on.

When everyone left, she went into the kitchen. She saw the lunch box was on the slab so she lifted the box to put in the sink but it was heavy. So, she opened it and the delicious aroma of the Kheer hypnotized her. She couldn't control herself and she tasted it. It was yummy. She went to Rajat and asked," did you make this?" He nodded. She laughed and said," it is so yummy and everything is in perfect proportion and you remembered that I like Kheer. You remembered..." "Yes, I remembered," he said, smiling. "Thank you for making my birthday the best birthday ever." " Actually, half credit goes to my mother. She encouraged me to do something for you."

"Really?" She asked.

"Yes, she told me that you are upset these days. So, I thought if you talk to your friends and eat your favourite dish then it will make you happy," Rajat said.

" I will say thanks to mom tomorrow and thank you for caring for me so much. I am lucky to have a family like this."

Leela said, and her perfect day ended but brought a new beginning of the happy days.

CHAPTER FIVE

The Voice of the Drawings

"Sometimes some situations break us but at that time we should think of the best day of our life and the things that make us happy and we should follow it."

Aditya and Guneet were blessed with a baby boy on 17th March,1997. They both loved him a lot and named him 'Anmol'. Aditya was a very rich businessman of Jamshedpur— the steel city of India. He made a good work-life balance. He bought various toys and games for Anmol. But he never responded to the sounds of the toys or his mother. Soon they understood that he was deaf. This news broke Aditya's heart but Guneet stayed strong and accepted the reality. On the other hand, Aditya wasn't ready to accept that his one and only child was deaf and slowly he engaged himself in so much of work that he didn't realize he had a family.

On the other hand, Anmol grew up and became close to his mother. Guneet and Anmol went together to the water park, zoo, and malls. Guneet used to draw and paint.

Similarly, Anmol developed an interest in drawing and painting. When he was 5, he made his first drawing, in which he was holding one hand of his mother and his other hand was open up in the direction of his father who was not looking at him. At that age, he made such a sensitive drawing. When he showed the drawing to his mother, Guneet hugged him tightly and kissed his cheeks. In the evening, when Aditya came back to the home, Guneet told him everything and showed the drawing, hoping that he might change his attitude towards Anmol. But he took the drawing and threw it away. Slowly, Anmol's drawing improved and those drawings became the only way of his communication and through them he expressed his feelings and desires.

Few years later, Guneet was diagnosed with leukemia. Anmol also observed that something was wrong with his mother. He drew a picture of his mother in which he was hugging her tightly but his father was forcefully breaking their hug. When he showed the drawing to Guneet, she couldn't stop her tears and by seeing her like that Anmol also started crying. After a few days, Anmol entered his mother's room, the room which became vacant recently. He slowly opened the drawer of the cupboard and saw a box on which Anmol's photo was pasted. He took the box and cried a lot. No one was able to calm him down. Soon a caretaker and a nurse took him away from the room and helped him sleep. The vacant house was filled by the caretaker and the nurse but no one was able to fill the void in Anmol's heart.

Next week, Aditya packed Anmol's things and left him at an orphanage home. Anmol was unexpectedly nub and he saw his father abandoning him at the reception of the orphanage home. He didn't react to anything and for months he didn't interact with anyone. He just lay down in his bed, curled up into a ball and hugged his box which his mother left for him. He hadn't opened it yet. He didn't draw anyone, in fact nobody in the orphanage knew that he could draw. Few months had passed and finally he drew a painting in which was asking to buy new crayons from a head lady of the orphanage who was very kind to everyone. He went towards the lady and poked on her hand, when she looked at him, he gave his painting to her. She saw the painting, smiled and put her hands on his head and nodded in response. For the first time he smiled after his mother died. And gradually his paintings became everyone's favourite.

On 17th March, 2018 he published his first book "**The voice of the Drawings**" of 300 pages, in which he just drew his life story. The book didn't contain any words but the drawings were more than enough to convey his journey. The book became the best-selling book and he became the author cum painter. After his book's success, he went into his home and opened that box. His eyes were filled with tears when he saw that his mother drew a painting of him in which he was holding his "book" on the stage and behind him a poster was hanging on which was written 'best seller book of the year by Anmol'.

CHAPTER SIX

Every House Says Something

> ***"Everyone is special because he or she has his or her own story. The house is made by us, so naturally, every house says something interesting, all we need is to listen to it."***

Keshav was a hardworking guy and he was always ready to learn something new from the environment and from the people. He worked as a postman. He loved to observe human behaviour and he wrote many poems and stories on the nature of humans in his free time. He was a married man and had a son.

Early in the morning, around 5 AM, he woke up with full energy and he was ready to learn new lessons from nature, humans and life. He got ready, washed his bicycle and ate breakfast with his son and left for his work with his son. First, he dropped his son to his school and then headed to the post office. This was his daily routine. He chose the same path to reach the post office. On that path, there was a house which was very old and it looked like nobody ever lived in that house for more than 25 years. The doors and windows were always closed in that ancient house. Keshav always saw that house and it always fascinated him. He used to think about the history of the house. On that day, he saw that a man and a little girl were standing outside that house. It looked like the little girl was the daughter of that man. The man was saying something to his daughter and occasionally indicating every window of the ancient house. The girl seemed to enjoy the tour of the house. Keshav stopped his bicycle near them and asked about the house. The girl replied that the house was of her great grandmother and her father used to live there when he was 5. Keshav smiled and said that the house was really very fascinating and beautiful. After this he continued his journey.

In the post office, he collected the letters and left from the post office to deliver them at their right places. Today the letters were less in numbers than that of the other days, so that means he could go home early. To deliver the first letter he reached his destination and knocked on the door. An old lady wearing a dark blue cotton saree, opened the door. Due to the scorching heat of the sun, Keshav asked for a glass of water from that lady. She invited him in and told Keshav to sit down for a bit. Keshav sat on a chair next to the television. The house was lit with a dim light bulb and there was a wall on which circles, squares and different shapes were drawn from the crayons. It was definitely the artistic work of a child. Curiously, Keshav asked about the doodling from the lady when he brought the glass of water. She smiled at his question but her smile reflected the painful story behind those drawings. She said that the drawings were a reminder of her son's childhood who died in a war, 7 years ago. Keshav wiped his tears and handed the letter to her and said with a heavy heart that her son is alive in each and every Indian heart.

After delivering all the letters, he was on his way back to his home. In the path he saw a woman was covering her hut with mud and her two kids were also helping her. They were not rich or hadn't had a big house but they enjoyed their work and their life. On reaching the home, Keshav wrote in his diary that, it doesn't matter if the house is new or old, brightly coloured aur dull, fully organized or messy, every house has its own identity and story. Old and dump walls have lots of memories, every window and door open a new path of memories and every mud-covered hut has its own aroma. '**Every house says something.**"

CHAPTER SEVEN

The Ray of Hope

"“Our life is like phoenix bird, we again born, rise, grow and develop into more beautiful version of ourselves from our own past experiences.”"

Mridula, a working woman, who was in her early 40s was sitting in her small cubical in her office and editing some designs of her presentation. She was alone in the office as it was mid-night and she was still working on her presentation which she had to present next morning to the client. Earlier she was very good at her work and she enjoyed doing her job but now she felt that she was stuck in that small cage link cubical. Mridula was extremely tired and suddenly she blanked out. She stopped editing, she stopped thinking and she just shut off the laptop. She couldn’t feel anything for a moment and then she realized that she stared hating her work which once she loved the most. She couldn’t see any progress in her life. She wanted to quit her job but she was confused about what if she took the decision emotionally and in future, she would regret taking it.

Sometimes our mind and our heart think different things. If, Mridula listen to her mind and she quit her job then people around her would speak that she doesn't care about her family conditions and she only thinks about her. And if she continues doing her job on the loop then she would go insane. She immediately booked a cab and went to her home where her husband and her 10 years old daughter sleeping peacefully. She made a cup of coffee and sat on the couch and took a deep breath. She took a sip of coffee and lost in its taste and she ride on a train which took her to a tour of her beautiful and always young memories. In that amazing journey, she found various speed breakers which stopped her from taking wrong decision, which she already took in her life. But all that speed breakers were the part of her life and now those speed breakers became her mentors. And in this 'memory tour' she took a turn and met with a hectic traffic jam. But this traffic jam made her realize that problems would come and go, all she need was to calm herself down, no matter how much noise pollution was caused by horns and the scorching heat of the sun took her exam of patience. After the traffic jam she would always find the smooth road that taught her the after hard work and patience, she always got happiness and mental peace. This tour wasn't simple journey but it was the educational tour of her life, from her life and for her life. She remembered all the forgotten faces, places, things, games, her litter secrets and pains, though this journey. She felt different kind of connection, a connection with herself, a connection of her younger version who was always ready to take risks and chances.

She woke up and realized that she was asleep for more than 6 hours and she felt very relaxed and her mind felt fresh. She decided to talk to her family about quitting her job and start a fresh work life with a lot of experiences.

About The Author

ABOUT THE AUTHOR

Sakshi is a student of B. Pharmacy at Banasthali Vidyapith, Jaipur after completing her schooling from D.A.V. Public School, Lalpania, Jharkhand. She wrote a book named "Bolti Kavitaye" as a co-author and also learned classical dance (Kathak). Now she finally stepped into the world of writing books as an independent author thought the book — *'Listen, what tales tell...'*.

Printed by Libri Plureos GmbH in Hamburg,
Germany